You're Growing Smaller and Smaller!

"Help! Help! I'm shrinking!" you yell.

Then suddenly you are only one inch high!

"Come over here!" calls a deep voice from under a bush. "I'll help you!"

Just then you see a white sneaker moving down the path. It is the foot of a giant boy.

If you hop on the sneaker, turn to page 4

If you go to the bush, turn to page 6.

**WHAT WILL HAPPEN NEXT?
TURN THE PAGE FOR
MORE THRILLS AND FUN!
WHATEVER YOU DO,
IT'S UP TO YOU!**

D1502445

WHICH WAY SECRET DOOR Books for you to enjoy

Available from ARCHWAY paperbacks

Most Archway Paperbacks are available at special quantity discounts for bulk purchases for sales promotions, premiums or fund raising. Special books or book excerpts can also be created to fit specific needs.

For details write the office of the Vice President of Special Markets, Pocket Books, 1230 Avenue of the Americas, New York, New York 10020.

which way · secret door · books #6

R.G. Austin

The Inch-High Kid

Illustrated by
Dennis Hockerman

AN ARCHWAY PAPERBACK
Published by POCKET BOOKS • NEW YORK

**For Heather and Sheila,
Jay and Debbie**

This novel is a work of fiction. Names, characters, places and incidents are either the product of the author's imagination or are used fictitiously. Any resemblance to actual events or locales or persons, living or dead, is entirely coincidental.

AN ARCHWAY PAPERBACK *Original*

 An Archway Paperback published by
POCKET BOOKS, a division of Simon & Schuster, Inc.
1230 Avenue of the Americas, New York, N.Y. 10020

Text copyright © 1983 by R. G. Austin
Illustrations copyright © 1983 by Pocket Books,
a division of Simon & Schuster, Inc.

All rights reserved, including the right to reproduce this book or portions thereof in any form whatsoever. For information address Pocket Books, 1230 Avenue of the Americas, New York, N.Y. 10020

ISBN: 0-671-46984-3

First Archway Paperback printing September, 1983

10 9 8 7 6 5 4 3 2 1

AN ARCHWAY PAPERBACK and colophon are trademarks of Simon & Schuster, Inc.

WHICH WAY is a registered trademark of Simon & Schuster, Inc.

SECRET DOOR is a trademark of Simon & Schuster, Inc.

Printed in the U.S.A.

IL   1+

ATTENTION!

READING A SECRET DOOR BOOK IS LIKE PLAYING A GAME.

HERE ARE THE RULES

Begin reading on page 1. When you come to a choice, decide what to do and follow the directions. Keep reading and following the directions until you come to an ending. Then go back to the beginning and make new choices.

There are many stories and many endings in this book.

HAVE FUN!

It is dark outside. You have gone to bed, but you are still wide awake.

You lie quietly until everyone in the house is asleep. Then you creep out of bed and tiptoe into the closet.

You push away the clothes and knock three times on the back wall. Soon the secret door begins to move. It opens just wide enough for you to slip through.

Turn to page 2.

As soon as you step through the door, you feel yourself growing smaller. And smaller. And smaller.

"Help! Help! I'm shrinking!" you yell.

"Come over here!" calls a deep voice from under a bush. "I'll help you!"

Just then you see a white sneaker moving down the path. It is on the foot of a giant boy.

If you hop on the sneaker, turn to page 4.

If you go to the bush, turn to page 6.

You leap onto the sneaker and grab a shoelace. The boy goes up some stairs and through a door. Then through another door. With every step, you bounce around.

Finally he stops walking.

Safe at last, you think.

You look around. You are in a bedroom. There is an empty candy wrapper on the floor. Suddenly you realize that you are hungry.

If I can get that boy's attention, maybe he will get me some food, you think.

If you try to climb up the boy's leg, turn to page 8.

If you try pulling on his shoelace so he will look down, turn to page 10.

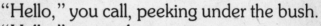

6

"Hello," you call, peeking under the bush.

"Hello," says a deep voice.

You look up into the huge, bulging eyes of a monster!

"Wh-who are you?" you ask. You are terrified!

"Me?" says the monster. "I'm a praying mantis."

"A bug?" you ask, horrified.

"Please remember your manners!" the mantis says. "I'm an insect, not a bug. Hop on my back and I'll take you for a ride."

You climb on.

"Here we go!" says the mantis. And he takes a huge leap. You love it!

This is almost like flying, you think.

Suddenly the mantis looks up. "Oh-oh," he says. "We're in trouble. Hold on!"

You look up. There is a huge bird flying right at you.

Turn to page 12.

You grab hold of the boy's jeans. Slowly, hand over hand, you pull yourself up.

Then, without warning, the boy sits down and crosses his legs.

Oh, no! You are falling!

You hit the ground and tumble across the room.

You stop rolling right in front of a log cabin. Next to the cabin is a bookcase. And right in front of both is a big, mean-looking cat!

If you run into the cabin, turn to page 22.

If you try to run under the bookcase, turn to page 24.

You untie the shoelace. Then you pull on it very hard. At first, the boy just wiggles his foot. You pull again. This time the boy looks down.

His eyes open wide in surprise. "Who are you?" he asks, startled.

"I'm just a regular kid," you yell. "But I've shrunk!"

"How did it happen?"

"I'm not quite sure," you yell. "But it did and I'm hungry!"

"I'll go get you some food," the boy says.

"Which do you want: Cherry Jell-O or strawberry yogurt?"

If you ask the boy for some Jell-O, turn to page 14.

If you would rather have him bring you some yogurt, turn to page 18.

You slide off and hide under a leaf. The bird flies away.

You are about to leave your hiding place when you feel something sticky all over your hand.

Oh, no! You are hiding on a spider's web!

The spider feels the web shake. She thinks she has trapped something. She is crawling right toward you!

If you try to run away, turn to page 16.

If you try to talk to the spider, turn to page 20.

The boy brings you a big bowl of Jell-O. He puts it next to you on the floor. Then he makes a staircase for you out of some thin books.

You look over the edge of the bowl at all the Jell-O. You have always wondered what it would be like to swim in Jell-O.

You bend your legs and jump right into the middle of the Jell-O. You bounce up. It is like jumping on a bed. You bounce some more. Then you float on your back. You wiggle and the Jell-O wiggles with you.

You turn your head and eat some Jell-O. Then you bounce and float some more. You have never had so much fun in your whole life.

The End

You try to get away. The sticky web clings to you.

"Hey!" the spider yells. "You're ruining my home! Please stop."

You stop. "I'm sorry," you say. "I didn't mean to ruin your web."

"A web is a spider's castle," she says. "I've worked too long on this home for it to be broken."

You look at the spider. You can tell that her feelings are hurt.

"I really *am* sorry," you say. "I won't hurt your house."

"In that case," the spider says, "Would you like to have a look around?"

If you want to tour the spider's web, turn to page 32.

If you thank the spider but tell her you must go now, turn to page 34.

The boy brings you some yogurt. You lean down and dip your hand into the creamy red stuff.

Uh-oh! You lean too far. You fall right into the yogurt. You are sinking!

You take a breath. But instead of air, you swallow yogurt.

Then suddenly you begin to grow!

Soon you are back to your own size. And the best part of it is, you have a new friend.

The End

Before you can say a word, the spider yells at you.

"What do you think you are doing?" she says.

"I'm sorry," you say. "I didn't mean to hurt anything."

"What kind of tasty morsel are you?" the spider asks.

"I'm a human," you answer.

"Don't be ridiculous," the spider says.

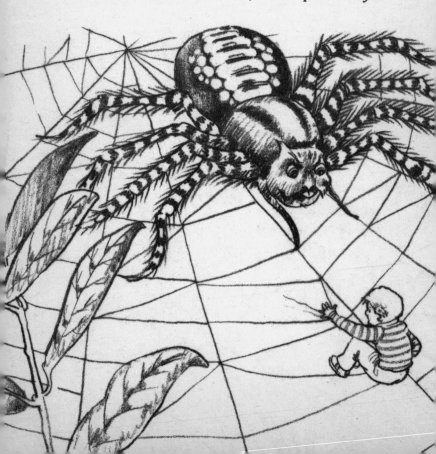

"It's true," you answer, "but I've shrunk."
"You'd still be good to eat," she says.
Now you're really scared! This spider thinks that you are her dinner!

If you tell the spider that you are too tough to eat, turn to page 25.

If you tell the spider you will bite her if she touches you, turn to page 30.

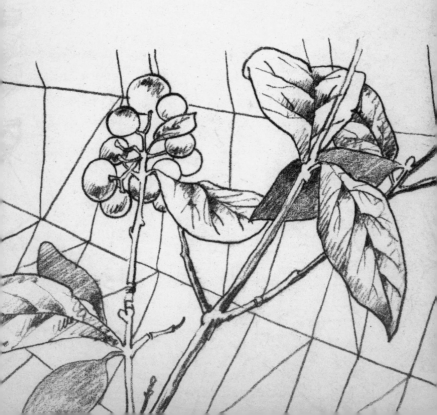

You run into the cabin and slam the door behind you.

"Whew!" you exclaim.

Then, to your surprise, you see a girl in the living room!

"Hi," she says. "Was that nasty cat chasing you?"

"Yes."

"That's the only bad thing about living here. Other than that, life is perfect. I would never leave this place."

"You mean you could go home if you wanted to?" you ask.

"Sure. But why should I leave? This place is fun. I don't have to clean my room. I don't have to carry out the garbage. And I never dry the dishes.

Turn to page 26.

You dash for the bookcase. But the cat reaches out and stops you. Then it bats you back and forth between its two front paws. It thinks you are a mouse.

If you try to tug the cat's fur to make it stop, turn to page 36.

If you talk to the cat, turn to page 40.

"You can't eat me," you say. "I'm too tough." You stick out your foot and touch your shoe. "See?"

The spider tries to take a bite of your shoe. "I guess you're right," she says. "You *are* too tough." Then she crawls sadly away.

Saved by a shoe! you think with a secret smile.

The End

"That sounds great to me," you say.

You stay in the cabin for a whole week. You go to bed when you want to. You eat when you feel like it. You do exactly what you please.

At first you love it. Then you start to get homesick. You miss your family. You miss your friends. You even miss your household chores. And yet you love being able to play all day.

You ask the girl how to get home. She tells you that your closet door is just down the path at the back of the yard.

"But you must go today," the girl says. "Tonight the door will be locked forever."

If you decide to stay, turn to page 28.

If you decide to go home, turn to page 38.

You love to play. And you play all day long.
You jump on the trampoline.

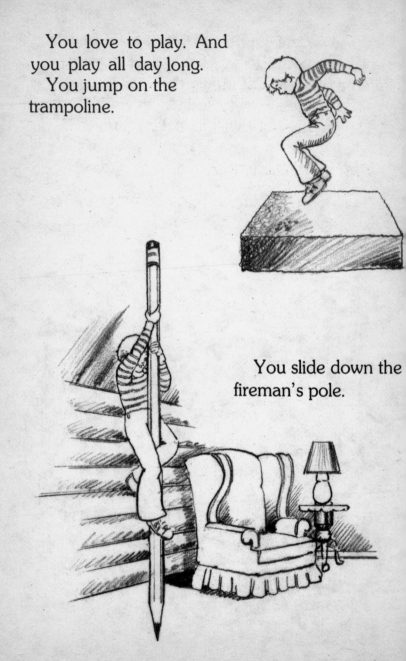

You slide down the fireman's pole.

You swim in the pool.

Every once in a while,
you think about home.

Turn to page 37.

"If you so much as touch me I'll bite you!" you say to the spider in a fierce voice.

"I'll bite you first," the spider says as she crawls closer to you.

"I'll bite first!"

"No! I'll bite first!" she says.

Suddenly everything seems silly. You start to giggle. Then the spider starts to giggle. Soon you are laughing together.

"That's really funny," the spider says. "I've never argued with a human before. And I've never had a human as a friend." Then she says shyly, "Will you be my friend?"

"Sure," you say. "That might be fun." And it is fun.

The End

"This is the living room," the spider says proudly.

"Very pretty," you say.

This doesn't look like a living room, you think.

"And this is the kitchen," the spider says. "My, that sink needs a good scrubbing."

I don't see a sink, you think. *What a stupid spider.*

"And this is the dining room," the spider says with a smile as she grabs you. "Gotcha!"

You were wrong. That spider was *not* so stupid after all!

The End

You wave good-bye to the spider. Then you walk across the grass. It seems as though you have traveled a long distance when you see a car ahead of you. It is the fanciest racing car you have ever seen.

You climb into the car and strap on your seat belt.

Suddenly you feel yourself moving.

"Look at it go," says a voice.

"Wow," says another.

Oh, no, you think. *I'm in somebody's remote-controlled car! I sure hope he knows how to work the controls.*

Turn to page 53.

The next time the cat hits you with its paw, you grab a tuft of fur and yank as hard as you can.

The cat feels an itch.

Scratch, scratch, scratch. He shakes his paw. He shakes it even harder.

Oops! You go flying across the room.

Well, you think, *tugging on his fur certainly didn't work. What now?*

You'd better go back to page 24 and make another choice.

After a couple of weeks, you are tired of playing. You think about home more and more. You wonder if you have made a mistake.

But it is too late. All day long there is nothing to do except play.

The End

You say good-bye to your friend. Before you know it, you are walking through your closet door. Soon your mother walks into your room.

"This place is a mess!" your mother says. "I want you to clean it up right now. And I don't want to hear any excuses!"

"Sure, I'll clean it up," you say with a smile.

Your mother stares at you. She looks worried. "Are you all right?" she asks.

The End

40

"Hey! Stop it, will ya!" you yell.

The cat stops and listens. Then it sticks its paw out again.

"No!" you scream even louder. "Can't you see I'm not a mouse! I'm a human!"

"You could have fooled me," says the cat. "I think I'll eat you anyway."

"If you do, I'll bite your tongue," you say.

"Then what should I do with you?" the cat asks.

"Help me," you say. "I need to be noticed by the boy. That's the only way I'll be saved. But I don't know what to do to get his attention."

If you ask the cat what you should do, turn to page 42.

If you ask the cat to take you to the boy, turn to page 44.

"I have an idea!" the cat says. "Let's leave your footprints all over the place. He'll certainly notice you then!"

"Maybe," you say.

You climb onto the cat's back. Then the cat jumps onto the boy's desk.

"See that Magic Marker?" the cat says. "Take off your shoes and socks and rub your feet on the inky part."

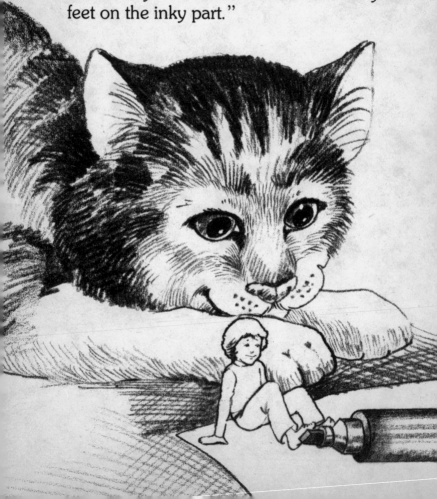

"Now," says the cat. "Walk all over that white piece of paper there."

You walk around on the paper. Then you move off the paper and wait.

Soon the boy comes to the desk.

"Drat!" the boy says when he sees his paper. "I'd better copy my homework over. It's too messy." He crumples the paper and throws it away.

If you try to make the footprints again, turn to page 46.

If you try to find another solution, turn to page 50.

The cat lies down on the floor. You climb onto its back.

Then the cat leaps onto the boy's lap.

"Goodness, Elmer!" the boy says to the cat. "That's the biggest flea I have ever seen!"

Then he picks you up and throws you away. You land in a paper cup.

Oh, no! you think. *I'm trapped.*

You try to climb the sides. But they are slippery.

I better think of some way to get out of here, you tell yourself.

If you scream at the top of your lungs, turn to page 48.

If you try running back and forth to attract attention, turn to page 56.

After the boy copies his homework, you make the black footprints all over the page again. Then you have an idea.

"Shove that magnifying glass on top of the paper," you tell the cat.

When the boy returns this time, he looks at his paper.

"What's going on here?" he asks.

Then he picks up the magnifying glass.

"Those are footprints!" he says. "And that," he adds looking at you, "is a kid!"

You have been saved!

The End

"Help!" you scream. "HELP ME!" you scream even louder.

The shape of the cup magnifies your voice.

A shadow appears over you.

"Who's there?" a voice booms at you.

"ME!" you scream. "I need help."

"Well, I'll be . . ." says the boy. "It's not a trick."

"Nope," you say. "I've shrunk. You have to help me grow big again."

"Well, it may take a while, he says, but we'll solve this problem together. I promise."

The End

You tell the cat to pick up the pen in his mouth. Then you show him what to draw.

The two of you work very hard. When you are finished, you have drawn the back side of your closet door.

You say thank you and good-bye to the cat. Then you open the door and return to your room. You are happy to be home. And you are even happier to see that you have grown back to your right size.

The End

CRASH!

You climb out of the smashed-up car.

Thank goodness I was wearing my seat belt, you think.

"Hey, Dumbo," you yell. "Why don't you learn how to drive?"

Luckily, the giant kid doesn't hear you.

The End

When you crawl out of the cup, you are standing in front of a typewriter. Suddenly you have an idea!

You climb onto the keys.

Carefully, you jump from one key to another. When you are finished, your message reads:

i am shrunk and i need help i will be on top.

You are so tired that you fall asleep. When you wake up, you are sitting in the hands of the boy.

That was a clever solution!

The End

You run across the cup and crash into the side. Then you run back and bump the other side.

The cup begins to sway back and forth. Then *crash!* The cup falls down.

Turn to page 54.

ATTENTION KIDS!

NOW THAT YOU'VE BEEN THROUGH THE SECRET DOOR, YOU'LL WANT TO RETURN AGAIN AND AGAIN.

Fast-paced action and loads of fun are yours as you walk through a secret door and enter lands of surprise, fantasy, and suspense.

In these books, you create your own story. What happens next is always up to you. Go to one page, you might meet a witch. Choose a different page, you might run into a sea monster. It's all up to you.

Outwit the dragon, play with the bear, behold the dinosaurs, giants, space creatures, magicians, and hundreds of other amazing characters.

Start your complete collection of these wonderful, illustrated stories by R.G. Austin right now.

#1 WOW! YOU CAN FLY! 46979/$1.95
#2 GIANTS, ELVES AND SCARY MONSTERS 46980/$1.95
#3 THE HAUNTED CASTLE 46981/$1.95
#4 THE SECRET LIFE OF TOYS 46982/$1.95
#5 THE VISITOR FROM OUTER SPACE 46983/$1.95
#6 THE INCH-HIGH KID 46984/$1.95

If your bookseller does not have the titles you want, you may order them by sending the retail price (plus 75¢ postage and handling—New York State and New York City residents please add appropriate sales tax) to: POCKET BOOKS, Dept. SEC, 1230 Avenue of the Americas, New York, N.Y. 10020. Send check or money order—no cash or C.O.D.s and be sure to include your name and address. Allow six weeks for delivery. For purchases over $10.00, you may use VISA: card number, expiration date and customer signature must be included.
674

Do You Know

WHICH WAY

To Go For Great Reading Adventures?

Go straight to these mystery and action-packed WHICH-WAY™ books—where **you** make the story go whichever way you want it to!

45756	$1.95	**THE CASTLE OF NO RETURN #1**
45758	$1.95	**VAMPIRES, SPIES AND ALIEN BEINGS #2**
45757	$1.95	**THE SPELL OF THE BLACK RAVEN #3**
43920	$1.95	**FAMOUS AND RICH #4**
44110	$1.95	**LOST IN A STRANGE LAND #5**
44189	$1.95	**SUGARCANE ISLAND #6**
45098	$1.95	**CURSE OF THE SUNKEN TREASURE #7**
45097	$1.95	**COSMIC ENCOUNTERS #8**
46021	$1.95	**CREATURES OF THE DARK #9**
46020	$1.95	**INVASION OF THE BLACK SLIME AND OTHER TALES OF HORROR #10**
46732	$1.95	**SPACE RAIDERS AND THE PLANET OF DOOM #11**

If your bookseller does not have the titles you want, you may order them by sending the retail price (plus 75¢ postage and handling for each order; NYS and NYC residents please add appropriate sales tax) to: Pocket Books, Dept. 2WW, 1230 Avenue of the Americas, New York, N.Y. 10020. Send check or money order—no cash or COD's please—and be sure to include your name and address. Allow up to six weeks for delivery. For purchases over $10.00 you may use VISA: card number, expiration date and customer signature must be included.

638

 ARCHWAY PAPERBACKS FROM **POCKET BOOKS**